LETTERS HOME

from

CANADA

Marcia S. Gresko

BLACKBIRCH PRESS, INC.
WOODBRIDGE, CONNECTICUT

Published by Blackbirch Press, Inc.
260 Amity Road
Woodbridge, CT 06525

©2000 by Blackbirch Press, Inc.
First Edition

e-mail: staff@blackbirch.com
Web site: www.blackbirch.com

Printed in Singapore

10 9 8 7 6 5 4 3 2 1

All photographs ©Corel Corporation

Library of Congress Cataloging-in-Publication Data
Gresko, Marcia S.
Canada / by Marcia S. Gresko.
    p.   cm. — (Letters home from . . .)
Includes bibliographical references and index.
Summary: Describes some of the sights and experiences on a trip to Canada, including visits
to Ottawa, Toronto, Montreal, and Quebec City.
ISBN 1-56711-410-5
1. Canada—Juvenile literature. [1. Canada—Description and travel.] I. Title. II. Gresko,
Marcia S. Letters home from—
F1008.2 .G74 2000   99-049710
973—dc21   CIP

TABLE OF CONTENTS

Arrival in . . .

Ottawa

It was a short trip to Ottawa, the capital city of Canada. We're spending the whole summer traveling in Canada because it's enormous—the second-largest country in the world after Russia. Canada has 10 provinces (like states) and 3 immense territories. They cover the northern half of North America and cross 6 time zones!

According to my guidebook, there are towering mountains, grassy plains, fertile farmlands, vast forests, bare arctic wastelands, and millions of lakes and rivers. There are thundering waterfalls, giant glaciers, and even a cool, misty rain forest. And when we're done enjoying the beautiful countryside, there are fun festivals to attend and large, lively cities to explore.

It's going to be a great summer!

Ottawa

Yesterday we rented bicycles and pedaled to Parliament Hill. In front of the grand Parliament buildings where Canada's laws are made, we watched the Changing of the Guard ceremony. The colorful event reminded us that Canada was ruled by Great Britain for more than a century.

Then we were off to Byward Market. Workers from the city's government offices, businesses, and industries joined tourists like us in the 150-year-old market. There were stalls piled with fruits, vegetables, and flowers. Ontario, the province in which Ottawa is located, has about half of Canada's richest farmlands. Shops sold meats, seafood, baked goods, and cheeses.

Downtown Ottawa

Night view of Parliament Hill

Barrel jumping at Winterlude

Flower vendor at market

We brought a picnic lunch to a park along the Rideau Canal. The guidebook says that during the winter it becomes the world's longest skating rink!

Today we visited some of the city's important museums. At the modern, National Gallery of Canada—made of glass and granite—we saw such amazing art! There were paintings from all over the world, sculptures by the country's native peoples, and in one of the courtyards—a rebuilt 100-year-old church! The Canadian Museum of Nature had a great dinosaur collection, and the National Museum of Science and Technology had everything from really cool antique cars to huge old locomotives.

Toronto

Early the next morning, we traveled southwest to Toronto—Canada's largest city. Toronto is Canada's chief financial, industrial, and transportation center. Banks, insurance companies, and other financial institutions like the Toronto Stock Exchange (the fourth-largest in the world) crowd the downtown area. Thousands of factories produce food items, clothing, electronics, electrical equipment, paper, and wood products. The city's bustling port is one of Canada's most important. From there, the country ships its products all over the world.

Toronto, Ontario

Financial District

Skydome and CN Tower

But Toronto is not all business! The city is also a cultural center. The Toronto Symphony, Canadian Opera, and National Ballet of Canada are located here. There are fine museums, important universities, restaurants of all kinds, and lots of shopping. At the "Underground City" you can shop along miles of subterranean stores, eateries, fountains, and trees!

I held my breath as a glass elevator whisked us up the side of the soaring CN Tower—the world's tallest free-standing structure. What a view! We could even see inside the famous SkyDome—the world's first sports stadium with a retractable roof. We're going to see the Toronto Blue Jays play there tonight!

Toronto

Today we visited 50 countries without leaving the city! Our "passport" for this adventure was Toronto's International Caravan—a lively, 10-day festival that celebrates the peoples and cultures that live here. People from all over the world have immigrated to Canada, and the country is proud of its multicultural heritage.

Booths are set up in ethnic neighborhoods, which allows visitors to discover each community's traditions, foods, and arts. We sampled Greek baklava; painted Ukrainian Easter eggs, and learned to tie a sari (Indian dress). More people from different countries live in Toronto than anywhere else in Canada—not surprising since Toronto means "meeting place!"

Fishing on Lake Simcoe

Toronto skyline

Niagara Falls

Today we visited one of the world's seven great natural wonders—Niagara Falls. Located on the Niagara River, on the border between Ontario and New York state, Niagara Falls is actually made up of two waterfalls. Horseshoe Falls is on the Canadian side and American Falls is on the U.S. side. Horseshoe Falls is a lot larger—about a half mile wide and more than 170 feet high. Millions of tourists like us visit each year, but the falls are also an important source of hydroelectric (water) power for both the U.S. and Canada. All I can say is wow!

Niagara Falls

Montreal

Bonjour (hello) from Montreal, the second-largest French-speaking city in the world after Paris, France! Because both the English and the French played such an important part in the country's early history, Canada has two official languages: English and French. Our guide explained that this has often caused problems, especially in Quebec (Canada's biggest province) where Montreal is located. Some French-speaking people want to separate from Canada and form their own country!

Skyline from Mount Royal

Montreal skyline

St. Paul Street

Notre Dame Cathedral

Montreal is the country's second-largest city. Nearly 80% of Canadians live in cities, most within 100 miles of Canada's border with the United States. Montreal is located on an island in the St. Lawrence River. Its location has made it an important port and trading center ever since it was founded by French fur traders more than 350 years ago.

In the middle of the island is Mount Royal. The city was named after and built around this mountain. From the top we saw a modern downtown, historic old neighborhoods, and large factories. Montreal's industries produce food, petroleum products, clothing, tobacco, and transportation equipment. The bustling harbor transports these goods all over the world.

Montreal Culture

We've been getting around Montreal on its amazing Metro. It's been called "the largest underground art gallery in the world!" Stations are decorated with everything from mosaics to stained glass.

This morning our destination was Old Montreal. Montreal is a leading cultural center with well-known dance, drama, and musical groups. There are elegant art galleries, an outstanding library system, and some of the country's best museums. At the Museum of Archaeology, we "talked" with the ghost-like holograms (images) of figures from the past!

Folk dancers, St. Jean Baptiste Church

Entertainer in Jacques Cartier Square

Botanical Gardens

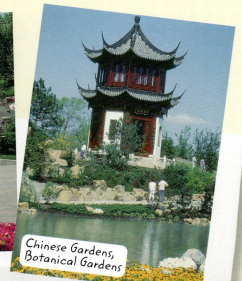
Chinese Gardens, Botanical Gardens

The city has more than 300 churches and many beautiful parks. The Botanical Gardens are among the largest in the world. There's a poisonous plant garden and the cool Insectarium, with more than 250,000 creepy crawly specimens! Yesterday, a horse-drawn carriage guided us around Mount Royal Park, the city's largest. It was designed by the same architect who created New York's Central Park.

Jacques Cartier Square, the heart of Old Montreal, is nearly 200 years old. Narrow cobblestoned streets are lined with historic buildings, colorful shops, and busy cafes. The jugglers, musicians, and mimes got us in the mood for tonight's treat—a performance of Montreal's famous Cirque du Soleil. It's like seeing a play and a circus all in one!

Quebec City

We traveled about 180 miles northeast to Quebec City. Founded by French explorer, Samuel de Champlain, the city is Canada's oldest. The United Nations has declared it a World Heritage site. Visiting Quebec City is like traveling to two cities at once! It's actually built on two levels!

Historic Upper Town is surrounded by 400-year-old walls, making it the only walled city in North America. Within the walls are grand government buildings, monuments, and parks. There are also fashionable shops, elegant restaurants, and luxury hotels. Ours looks like a fairytale castle! Nearby is the city's most famous landmark, a massive British fort called the Citadel.

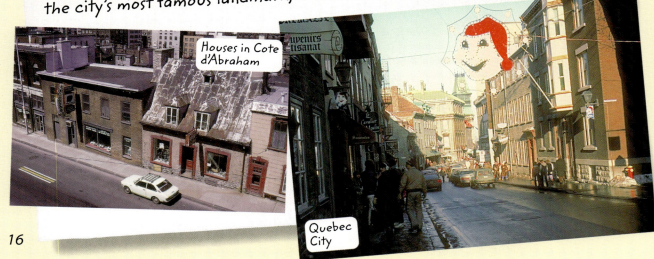

Houses in Cote d'Abraham

Quebec City

Ice castle

Passenger and car ferry

Southwest of the Citadel, located in Battlefields Park, are the Plains of Abraham. This is where the English finally defeated the French for control of Canada. But today, most Quebeccers have French ancestors and the city is a center of French Canadian culture and tradition. Lower Town includes Quebec City's industrial and business sections.

Today we took a sightseeing boat on the St. Lawrence River, part of the great St. Lawrence Seaway. It's a 2,400-mile-long system of locks, canals, and channels that link the Great Lakes with the Atlantic Ocean—allowing huge ships to enter the heart of Canada.

Winnipeg

Our next stop was Winnipeg, the capital of Manitoba. Our guidebook calls Winnipeg the "gateway to the west." That's because its location, halfway between the Atlantic and Pacific oceans, makes it the chief transportation link between eastern and western Canada. Winnipeg is also an important industrial center. More than 1,000 factories produce transportation and farm equipment, furniture, clothing, and processed foods.

Winnipeg looks kind of like some midwestern U.S. cities. Its downtown area has modern office buildings, hotels, shops, the Civic Center and art gallery, two universities, and a large sports stadium. We spent the day at the Centennial Arts Center, visiting the natural history museum and planetarium and enjoying a performance by th Royal Winnipeg Ballet.

Winnipeg

Saskatoon

We stopped in Saskatoon, the largest city in the province of Saskatchewan. This province, like Manitoba and Alberta, is a "prairie province." It's called the "bread-basket of Canada" because its flat prairies are perfect for growing wheat.

There's not much to see in Saskatoon, but we did enjoy the Western Development Museum with its stores, cars, and farm equipment that re-creates life a century ago. And the Ukrainian Museum was cool. Many Ukrainians, Germans, Romanians, Belgians, Austrians, and other Europeans immigrated to the prairie provinces in the early 1900s. That's when the Canadian government offered free land to help settle the vast western part of the country.

The Great Sand Hills

People of Saskatchewan

Edmonton

It's beautiful here in Edmonton, the capital of Alberta. With more hours of sunshine than any other province, it's been nicknamed Sunny Alberta. Another name for it is the "energy province" because it produces most of the country's oil and natural gas resources.

Our guide says millions of tourists enjoy Alberta's spectacular scenery each year. It's the largest of the prairie provinces. There are golden plains, snow-capped mountains, dense forests, and sparkling lakes. Alberta's spectacular wilderness areas are filled with a variety of wildlife. Visitors can go skiing, hiking, fishing and hunting, rafting, and horseback riding.

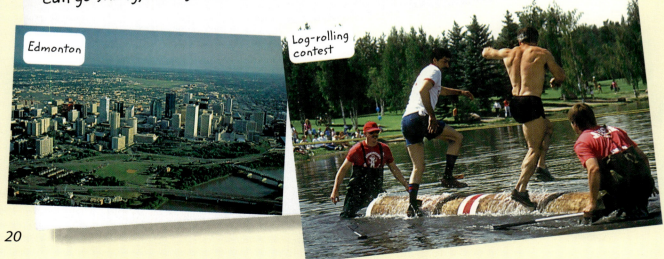

Edmonton

Log-rolling contest

Calgary

Wahooooo! We're in Calgary for the Calgary Stampede—the world's largest rodeo. It's a 10-day celebration of bronco riding, steer wrestling, and calf roping. There are chuck wagon races, wild cow milking contests, and parades!

Today we took a break from the rodeo to explore the city. We visited a zoo, museums, botanical gardens, and Olympic Park—built for the events of the 1988 Winter Olympics. We also saw Heritage Park—a frontier village where more than 100 old buildings from all over Canada have been re-created. Costumed staff "work" in the trading post, church, and school.

Tomorrow we're off to the nearby Drumheller area. It's known for its dinosaur fossils and weird, mushroom-like rock formations called hoodoos.

Calgary Stampede Rodeo

Calgary skyline

Vancouver

From Calgary we traveled southwest to Vancouver, British Columbia. "B.C." (as Canadians call it) is Canada's westernmost province and its third-largest. B.C. has more kinds of scenery than any other province. There are rolling farmlands, a rugged coastline dotted with offshore islands, a desert, icy mountain peaks, lakes, rivers, and the world's largest temperate rain forest.

Vancouver is the most beautiful city we've visited so far. Its modern skyscrapers soar between snowcapped mountains and the sparkling Pacific Ocean. There are parks and gardens everywhere. Stanley Park is a rain forest, and one of the world's largest city parks. We rented bikes to explore its tree-shaded trails, zoo, aquarium (with whales!), and beaches.

Vancouver

Chinatown

Granville Island

From our downtown hotel we can walk to interesting museums, historic buildings, trendy shops, and great restaurants. Nearby are towering banks, offices, and important government buildings. Cruise liners and cargo ships dock in the neighboring harbor. The busy downtown scene reminded us that Vancouver is an important cultural, business, and industrial center, as well as Canada's major seaport.

Yesterday we took the ferry to Granville Island. Sawmills, factories, and warehouses have been converted to restaurants, artists' studios, and a huge farmers' market. Today we took the bus to Chinatown, the second-largest in North America. The Chinese first came to Canada more than 100 years ago to build the railroads.

Yukon Territory

We flew nearly 1,500 miles north to Whitehorse, the capital of the Yukon Territory. Located on the Yukon River, Canada's second-longest river, Whitehorse was a rest stop for thousands of prospectors heading north to Gold Rush territory. Mining is still the area's most important industry.

Kluane National Park, about 100 miles west of Whitehorse, is awesome! We took a helicopter ride over enormous glaciers, ice fields, lakes, and forests. Our pilot pointed out Dall sheep, caribou, moose, and grizzly bears below! We also saw Mt. Logan, Canada's tallest mountain (19,550 ft). I can see why the native people named their home Yukon—which means "greatest."

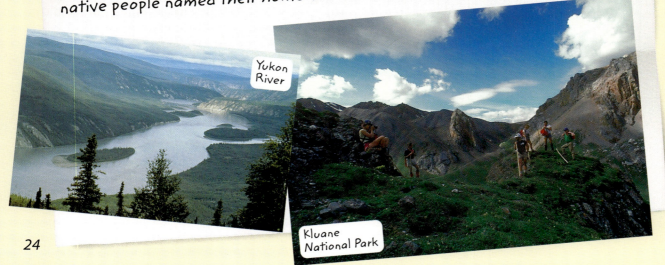

Yukon River

Kluane National Park

Northwest Territories

It's a beautiful sunny <u>night</u> here in Yellowknife, the capital of the Northwest Territories (usually called NWT). Because of its extreme northern location, the area gets about 20 or more hours of sunlight each day during the summer!

In 1999, a new territory—Nunavut—was created from part of the NWT. Nunavut, which means "our land," is governed by the Inuit—the area's native people. The only way to get to our rafting trip in Nahanni National Park was by small plane or helicopter. The scenery was incredible—canyons, rapids, hot springs, mountains, and waterfalls. Nunavut's Virginia Falls is twice as high as Niagara Falls!

First Canyon, Nahanni River

The Sluice Box

Newfoundland

Our next stop was Newfoundland's capital city, St. John's. Newfoundland, the easternmost province of Canada, is made up of the island of Newfoundland and the coast of Labrador, a part of mainland Canada. In summer, thousands of icebergs float south from the Arctic past Newfoundland!

We saw a Viking settlement, fishing villages, lighthouses, and the "sticks and stones house" (made of more than 50,000 popsicle sticks!). St. John's has museums, night spots, and shops featuring some of the area's crafts— hand-knitted clothing, carvings, sculpture, jewelry, and baskets. Most people work in service industries or in fishing, mining, and manufacturing.

Petty Harbor

Petty Harbor

Prince Edward Island

Have you read "Anne of Green Gables" or seen the movie? The author, Lucy Maud Montgomery, lived here and described the island's cliffs, beaches, and rolling hills in her book. Prince Edward Island is the smallest province—about the size of Delaware. It has fewer people than any other province, but because it's so tiny, it's the most crowded of them all!

We're staying in Charlottetown, the capital. Yesterday we visited historic Province House and saw the "Birthplace of Canada." Our guide explained that it was here that the union of Canada was planned. At dinner we ate two island specialties—lobster and potatoes! Lots of seafood is caught in the island's waters. And more than 70 kinds of potatoes are grown in the rich, red soil that has given the island the nickname the "million acre farm!"

Cape Tryon

New London Wharf

New Brunswick

Exploring New Brunswick is a real adventure! Most of the small province is unsettled and covered by forests. The north is mountainous, and the west is fertile farmlands watered by rushing rivers. The mostly rugged coastline has a few white sand beaches and scenic fishing villages. The province's two main cities are Fredericton, the capital, and St. John, its main port. That's where we've been staying.

Guess what I ate yesterday—seaweed! The purple seaweed (called dulse) is gathered at low tide in the Bay of Fundy. Then it's dried and eaten like potato chips or added to casseroles and soups.

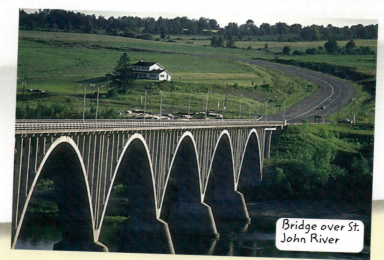

Bridge over St. John River

Oak Bay

St. John's Harbor

The Bay of Fundy separates the provinces of New Brunswick and Nova Scotia, the last stop on our trip. The bay has the highest tides in the world—as tall as a four-story building. In some places the powerful tides have carved strange shapes like the "Giant Flowerpots." One day we took a ferry to Deer Island, one of the three islands in the middle of the bay. Offshore at Deer Point we saw the "Old Sow," the world's second-largest whirlpool.

Can you guess what I'm bringing you from St. Stephen, the town where the guidebook says the chocolate bar was invented?

Nova Scotia

Hello from Halifax, the capital of Nova Scotia, our last stop for the summer. Located on a peninsula, the city is an important center of the shipping and fishing industry. Its modern, deep-water harbor is one of the best natural harbors in the world. Huge ships fill the harbor, exporting the province's fish, lumber, agricultural, and manufactured products. In the restored warehouses around it are lively pubs (bars), great restaurants, and trendy shops. The city also has pretty parks and gardens, museums and art galleries, more than a half dozen colleges and universities, and a huge star-shaped fort—the Citadel.

Peggy's Cove

Lighthouse at Peggy's Cove

Halifax Harbor Bridge

Cape Breton fisherman

According to a legend told by the area's native peoples, a mighty chief named Glooscap shaped the coastline of Nova Scotia and created its first peoples and animals. The province, whose name means "new Scotland," looks a lot like the country after which it was named. There are rugged highlands and fertile lowlands, flower-filled valleys, wooded hills, and lots of lakes and streams. Hundreds of small protected coves once made great hiding places for pirates. Captain Kidd's treasure is rumored to be buried here! I'm sending this letter from the post office at Peggy's Cove—the only Canadian post office located in a lighthouse!

Glossary

Ethnic to do with a group of people sharing the same origin or culture.

Fertile land that is good for growing crops.

Glacier a huge sheet of ice found in mountain valleys or polar regions.

Lock a part of a canal with gates at each end where boats are raised and lowered to different water levels.

Prospector an explorer, usually looking for gold or silver.

Province a district or region of some countries.

Subterranean under the ground.

For More Information

Books

Kalman, Bobbie. *Canada: The People* (The Lands, People, and Cultures). New York, NY: Crabtree Publishing, 1993.

Law, Kevin J. Sandra Stotsky. *Canada* (Major World Nations). New York, NY: Chelsea House, 1997.

Sylvester, John. *Canada* (Country Fact Files). Chatham, NJ: Raintree/Steck Vaughn, 1996.

Web Site

Canadian Culture

Links to information on Canadian history, heritage, art, government, and lifestyle—ace.acadiau.ca/Polisci/aa/digagora.Gallery/culture.html

Index